The Poky Little Puppy and the
PATCHWORK BLANKET

Story and pictures by
JEAN CHANDLER

GOLDEN PRESS • NEW YORK
Western Publishing Company, Inc., Racine, Wisconsin

Four little puppies, out for a walk, stopped to wait for their poky little brother, who was lagging behind as usual.

"He might not be so slow if he didn't drag that blanket everywhere," said one little puppy.

"I think I hear him crying," said another puppy.

Sure enough, the poky little puppy was crying and tugging at his blanket, which was caught on a fence.

"I was just taking a shortcut through the wide place in the fence, but my blanket got caught and won't come through," he sniffled.

"Don't cry. We'll help you!" said his brothers and sisters. "All together, now!"

Five little puppies pulled and pulled and pulled the blanket. Suddenly it tore loose, and they all tumbled down in a heap.

The poky little puppy was so happy to have his blanket that he didn't even notice the hole in one corner.

That night the poky little puppy came home long after his brothers and sisters. When his mother saw the big hole in his blanket, she was very displeased. While the poky little puppy ate his dinner, Mother mended the blanket.

"Don't ever take this blanket outdoors again," she scolded.

BUT . . . the very next day, that naughty puppy ran out dragging his blanket behind him!

Five little puppies went happily on their way, sniffing at this and looking at that. They sniffed at the raccoon footprints in the mud near the goldfish pool.

They looked at the goldfish
swimming in the clear water.

Then they ran up a little hill and down the other side to
the duck pond—one, two, three, four little puppies.
"Where is that poky little puppy now?" they wondered.

They found the poky little puppy back over the hill, trying to pull his blanket out of a prickly raspberry bush. When he saw his brothers and sisters he said, "These raspberries looked so good that I wanted to eat some, but my blanket got caught on the bush!"

"I guess we'll have to help him again," said one little
puppy. "All together, now!"

Five little puppies pulled and pulled and pulled the
blanket. Suddenly there was a tearing sound, and they
all went heels over head as the blanket came away from
the thorny bush.

There were two more holes in the blanket now!

That night, as Mother mended the blanket, she said,
"No dessert for puppies who tear their blankets. And
don't *ever* take this blanket outdoors again!"

Just the same, when the puppies went for their walk
the next day, the poky little puppy had his blanket with
him as usual.

And that blanket was a problem all day long.

It got caught on everything!
It got caught on rocks and stumps
and mailboxes.

It got caught on swings and seesaws and litter baskets.
Each time the puppies pulled and pulled to get it
loose. And each time another little bit was torn out of it.
The poky little puppy's blanket grew smaller and smaller.

That night Mother frowned and said, "It's too bad that you were so naughty. Now it looks as if there isn't enough of your blanket left to mend."

The poky little puppy tried every way he could think of to get under his blanket.

But no matter what he did, that blanket
was just too small to cover him.

He went to bed feeling
very sorry for himself.

The next day the poky little puppy sat looking sadly at the little scrap of cloth that had once been his blanket.

"Come with us," said his brothers and sisters. "Maybe we can find the missing pieces of your blanket, and then Mother can put them back together."

As the puppies brought in the scraps of orange cloth, they laid them out carefully, side by side, to see how they would fit together.

"There aren't enough pieces yet," said Mother. "You must find some more."

The puppies went out again and brought back as many bits and pieces as they could find.

"You are good little puppies," said Mother. "You have worked hard to find the pieces of Poky's blanket. But I'm afraid there still aren't enough pieces to make a whole blanket."

The poky little puppy looked very unhappy.

The little puppies thought hard about what to do next. They thought and thought, and then they thought some more.

Then one puppy had an idea. "My blanket is really much too big," he said. "You may have part of my yellow blanket, Poky."

"Poky may have some of my blue blanket, too," said
another puppy.

"Oh, please take some of my red blanket," said the
third little puppy.

"And some of my green one," said the fourth little
puppy.

That night, while the puppies were asleep, Mother
stitched all the pieces together. She even added some
scraps she had been saving to make a rug.

When the poky little puppy woke up the next morning he found a wonderful, warm patchwork blanket covering him.

"Oh," he said, "this is the most beautiful blanket in the whole wide world! Thank you, everybody! I will take very good care of this blanket always."

And after that, the poky little puppy never *ever* took his blanket outdoors again.